When Will I Fly?

by Laura Gates Galvin

Little Soundprints

Published by Soundprints Division of Trudy Corporation, Norwalk, Connecticut.

Book design: Bert Johnstone and Marcin D. Pilchowski
Editor: Ben Nussbaum
Production Editor: Brian E. Giblin

First Edition 2006
10 9 8 7 6 5 4 3 2 1
Printed in India

Peep and the Big Wide World is produced by WGBH and 9 Story Entertainment in association with TVOntario and Discovery Kids. Major funding for *Peep and the Big Wide World* is provided by the National Science Foundation.

This material is based upon work supported by the National Science Foundation under Grant No. 0104700. Any opinions, findings, and conclusions or recommendations expressed in this material are those of the author(s) and do not necessarily reflect the views of the National Science Foundation.

Library of Congress Cataloging-in-Publication Data
is on file with the publisher and the Library of Congress.

When Will I Fly?

by Laura Gates Galvin

Chirp, the robin, couldn't wait to learn how to fly.

"Try again," said Peep.
But Chirp was too discouraged. "That's it!" she said.
"I'm just not meant to be a flying bird."

"What kind of bird are you meant to be?" asked Peep.

"I don't know, but I'm going to find out," said Chirp.

"Well, I know that ducks are meant to be swimming birds. Goodbye!" said Quack, as he strolled back to his pond.

Chirp and Peep set out to learn what kind of bird Chirp was meant to be.

Frog hopped by.

Frog could hop high and he could hop far.

"A hopping bird? I am pretty good at hopping."

So Chirp hopped after Frog.

She hopped with all her might.

She hopped as far, and as long, and as well, as she could. But Frog was soon out of sight.

"I don't think I'm meant to be a hopping bird," sighed Chirp.

Later, as they walked down a hill, Chirp noticed a caterpillar.

She watched the caterpillar crawl smoothly along a leaf.

"Peep, maybe I'm meant to be a crawling bird!" she exclaimed.

Chirp lay down on the grass and crawled, wriggled, and squirmed with all her might.

Soon, Chirp was tired and sore. "Peep, I don't think I'm meant to be a crawling bird," she gasped.

Just then, Tom the cat ran by.

"He sure was running fast," said Peep.

"That's it! Maybe I'm meant to be a running bird!" said Chirp.

And just like that, she took off running.
Peep did his best to follow her.

After a while, Peep caught up to Chirp. Chirp was trying to catch her breath.

So, from that day forward, Chirp practiced flying like never before. And even though she still couldn't fly during the day, at night, in her dreams, she flew everywhere!

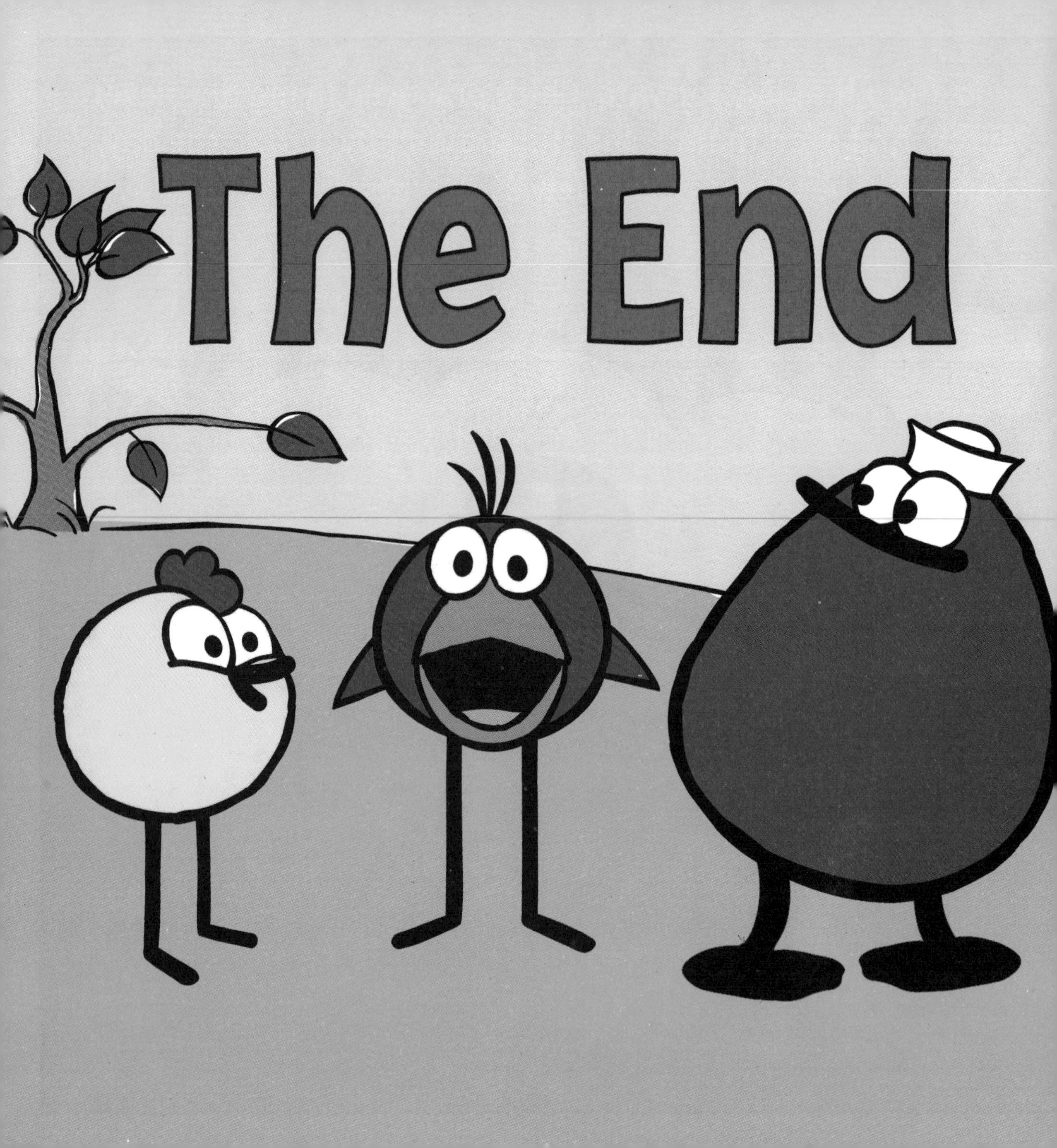
The End